DEMON
FROM THE DEEP END

JAMES ALLISON is the author of a number of science fiction and fantasy short stories, which have appeared in books and magazines as far afield as the UK, USA and Australia. Living and working in London, he is by day a mild-mannered proof reader and copy editor. By night he is even less heroic, preferring to hide indoors and dream up more scary ideas for books.

DEMON
FROM THE DEEP END

James Allison

Illustrated by
Dani Cruz

THE O'BRIEN PRESS
DUBLIN

First published 2009 by The O'Brien Press Ltd,
12 Terenure Road East, Dublin 6, Ireland.
Tel: +353 1 4923333; Fax: +353 1 4922777
E-mail: books@obrien.ie
Website: www.obrien.ie

ISBN: 978-1-84717-134-4

British Library Cataloguing-in-Publication Data
A catalogue record for this title is available from the British Library

1 2 3 4 5 6 7 8 9
09 10 11 12 13

The O'Brien Press
receives assistance from

Layout and design: The O'Brien Press Ltd
Printed in the UK by CPI Bookmarque, Croydon, CR0 4TD

For Ethan and Byron

Contents

1. A Holiday of Horrors

'Come on in, Liam,' greeted Evan Crogan's mum cheerily. 'He's in his room, you can go right up. Mind the brains on the stairs.'

Gripping the rolled holiday brochure in his fist, Liam scooted up the stairs to Evan's bedroom door, where a large 'DO NOT DISTURB' sign hung over a colourful home-made movie poster for *Revenge of the Killer Snails II*.

Even in a house where you had to be ready for

anything, he still jumped back in surprise as a towering, tentacled mutant suddenly burst from the room. The creature grunted a muffled 'Yo, Liam' before it skidded on a rubber brain, bounced down the stairs and staggered away, swearing loudly as its huge wobbly head took out a ceiling light.

'I see you got your bro playing the monster again,' noted Liam, poking his head into Evan's room.

It was no surprise. Being the tallest kid in the neighbourhood, Evan's brother always got to play the monster. Most of the neighbours didn't even look twice now when they spotted him lumbering about the garden with fountains of bright green blood spurting out of him.

'The evil Lord Krengor was about to meet his doom by gamma radiation bombardment,' grumbled Evan, sitting cross-legged on the floor, eyes still glued to the viewing screen of his camcorder. 'But he had to go to rugby practice.'

He sighed and shook his head, clearly infuriated that something as mindless as *sport* was

interfering with his movie-making schedule.

Liam removed a half-eaten cheeseburger and a plastic chainsaw from a beanbag and flopped down.

'Ever think about going abroad for some location shooting?' he suggested. 'Maybe somewhere a bit exotic and unusual?'

'Abroad?' queried Evan, warily. With his pasty-white skin and wispy red hair, Evan looked like he would dissolve if he ever saw sunshine.

'My dad's got a last-minute DJ gig in a Spanish hotel. It's a tiny place, looks really quiet. You can come along if you like, it's only for a few days before half-term ends.'

'Is your sister going?'

'Yeah, but she'll just sit inside and do puzzles or something, she won't bother us. She's forgiven you now anyway.'

Evan flinched at the memory. He had once tried to persuade Sophie Brodie to appear as an extra in *School for Zombies*, only for her to tell him where he could shove his camera. And his plan to film her anyway had ended badly after he'd lurched in front of her as a rotting ghoul. Her scream had been genuine all right, but definitely not worth the beating he'd taken.

'Check it out,' said Liam, offering the opened holiday brochure. 'Kind of creepy-looking, I reckon.'

Evan pored over the pictures of the hotel for a moment, his eyes widening as he scanned the images.

'This is not bad,' he enthused. 'I could definitely get some footage for *Breakfast for the Undead* here.'

'You're up for it then?' beamed Liam.

'Well, I'll have to write a shooting script for the film first. And I'll need to ask my mum if I can go. And sun cream, of course – I'll need *serious* amounts of sun cream.'

'Great! I'll let my dad know. We're flying on Thursday, better get your stuff ready.'

'Are you *sure* your sis isn't mad at me anymore?' added Evan.

'Don't worry, it'll be just fine,' soothed Liam.

Evan looked unconvinced.

When Liam picked up the brochure to leave, he was too excited to notice that the photos of the hotel pool seemed to be shimmering slightly, as though the water was rippling on the page.

*   *   *

'I still can't believe you had to invite *him* along,' hissed Sophie to Liam for about the tenth time, her nose wrinkling in disgust.

Liam sighed. His plan to bring Evan on the trip hadn't exactly gone well so far. Especially on the plane, when his *Idiot's Guide to Making Monster Guts from Sausages* had fallen onto a fellow passenger's lap, making the man reach for his sick bag. Now they were in a midnight taxicab to the hotel, Liam could tell from his sister's expression that things weren't about to get any easier.

'Seems a long way from the coast for a resort,' said Liam's dad, as they watched the brightly-lit Spanish shoreline fade to dark and mountainous countryside.

'People not come here so much,' said the driver in a thick accent. 'And when they do, sometimes they not come back.'

'Oh, really? I guess they must like it here then.'

Liam and Evan glanced at each other, while Sophie winced as an enormous yellow insect splattered against the window.

A further ten minutes' driving brought them to the bottom of a steeply-sloping dirt road, with high stone walls on either side.

'Okay, only crazy peoples go further,' announced the driver, drawing the cab to a sudden halt. 'Bye-bye.'

'Dad!' wailed Sophie, as the driver began dumping their suitcases by the roadside. 'Do something! There are giant bugs everywhere, we'll be eaten alive!'

'This is just like Transylvania,' whispered Evan

to Liam. 'The local peasants always flipped out near Dracula's castle.'

The four of them watched in dismay as the taxicab pulled away into the night, leaving only a hazy moon to show the road ahead.

'Don't worry, kids,' reassured Liam's dad. 'We'll just have to make the best of it, it can't be too far.'

'Let's send Evan first,' said Sophie. 'He's so gross the bugs will probably just die if they eat him.'

'There's no scientific basis for that at all,' snapped Evan.

'We'll walk together,' said Liam's dad. 'It's safer that way.'

The hill proved hard work with the luggage to carry and Sophie shrieking every time she heard the buzz of wings near her. Nobody wanted to think about what was making the sickly crunching sounds under their feet.

At the top of the road, a set of tall iron gates appeared, the only opening in a pale wall that was almost covered in creeping vines. Beyond the gates, it was possible to see the outline of a large building looming from the darkness.

'Well done everybody,' said Liam's dad, pressing a buzzer on the gates. 'This looks like the place.'

Evan leaned over to Liam as the gates creaked open. 'Watch your back,' he whispered. 'Their greatest weapon is always surprise.'

Liam gulped as the four of them entered the grounds, the ghostly apartment blocks rising from thick and tangled clumps of vegetation that had a sickly-sweet odour.

The entire hotel appeared to be in darkness. The only light came from the large lagoon pool in the middle of the grounds, its murky waters glowing under blue lanterns.

'Not too bad really,' said Liam's dad bravely.

The shadowy figure that suddenly stepped into the pathway drew an intake of breath from them all. Sophie issued one of her famously shrill screams while Evan immediately assumed his vampire-killer kung-fu defence pose.

'Ah, excellent,' rasped the crooked figure, rubbing its spindly hands together. 'You've *arrived.*'

2. The Secret of the Pool

'Watch if we go past any mirrors,' Evan advised, as they followed the strange character who'd greeted them. 'If you can't see his reflection we're in trouble. I'll try and see if he photographs – the Undead usually don't.'

The man leered as he beckoned them on. Wearing a maroon and gold waistcoat and glossy boots, he had a waxy pencil moustache, veiny see-through skin and dead-fish eyes. He'd introduced himself as the hotel manager, but Liam thought he looked more like a cross between a circus ringmaster and a grumpy tadpole.

Evan was still grappling with his camcorder as the manager led them into a small reception area with dark-stained chairs and immense cobwebs hanging from the ceiling.

Spotting a large beetle scuttling across the reception desk, the manager snatched the insect into his mouth and noisily crunched on it.

Sophie looked like she was going to throw up.

'We keep the cleanest hotel here!' boasted the manager, a beetle leg still hanging from the corner of his mouth. 'No bugs in our kitchens!'

'Dad,' moaned Sophie, her face still green, 'I don't like Spain.'

'It will be good to have music playing here,' leered the manager. 'It will bring new *life*.'

Liam caught Evan stuffing a clove of garlic into his mouth.

'I'm going to smell so bad that *nothing* will want to eat me,' he mumbled.

Liam didn't think he smelled that great to begin with. Pulling his grubby old trainers off would probably have done the job.

'Can't wait to get started,' beamed Liam's dad. 'Where are we playing?'

The manager opened a door from the reception area to show them the entertainments hall. The room beyond appeared to be a large, darkened ballroom, the air thick with dust. Liam saw that tables and chairs had been laid out on the dance floor, and that some guests were sitting in silence, their faces blank, their eyes glassy.

'Tough crowd,' observed Liam's dad. 'Reckon I should be able to get them going with a few good tunes though.'

'Excellent,' said the manager, clasping his hands. 'But it's very late, you should perhaps go to bed and start tomorrow, yes?'

Evan kept filming with his camcorder as the manager led them through a series of corridors, each one darker and gloomier than the last, as though they were tunnelling into the depths of an ancient tomb. A small flight of steps finally brought them onto their floor, the manager bidding them a peaceful night before lolloping away.

'Dad, are we seriously not freaking out yet?' asked Liam.

'Place just needs a lick of paint, that's all,' said Liam's dad cheerily. 'Your man with the beetle habit back there seemed a bit strange, but I'm sure everything will be fine when the sun's out.'

Nobody looked very convinced about that, but with nowhere else to go, staying the night seemed the least scary option.

'Better watch out for booby-traps,' said Liam, as he warily entered his and Evan's room.

'It's just a good thing for you that I'm here, that's all,' said Evan, busily wedging a chair under the door handle. 'If we're going to do battle with evil forces you're going to need an expert.'

Liam watched as Evan unpacked his luggage, pulling out various vials and potions and a large wooden stake, which he stuffed under his pillow. He sat down by the door and waited until Liam had got into his bed before turning out the light, listening carefully for any sounds in the corridor.

Liam was just about to start snoozing when a thunderous fart vibrated across the floorboards.

'Evan, that totally stinks,' he complained.

'It's my garlic defence system,' whispered Evan. 'I'll try and squeeze a few more out. It'll stop any vampires coming in.'

Liam nodded off to sleep thinking that vampires were very sensible.

*   *   *

'Liam! Wake up! *Quick*!'

At Evan's urgent call, Liam awoke into darkness and began flailing in panic, finally landing in a tangled heap on the floor.

'Check this out,' said Evan, his voice hushed. 'There's something going on with the pool.'

Liam joined Evan at the grimy windows and gazed at the swimming pool, which seemed to be bubbling and spitting like a prehistoric swamp, great pockets of gas belching to the surface and loudly popping.

'This needs further investigation,' announced Evan, grabbing his camcorder.

'Are you nuts? Your horrible stink won't protect you out there!'

'First rule of supernatural combat,' explained Evan, 'always surprise them before they surprise you!'

Against his better judgement, Liam followed his friend from the room and through the twisting series of corridors down to the grounds.

Reaching the poolside, they hid behind some thick bushes and peered through the leaves as the water began to churn furiously.

'What if it's something like a giant man-eating frog that can slurp up its victims from twenty feet away?' asked Liam nervously.

'That's just silly,' dismissed Evan. He frowned

for a moment then pulled a small notebook from his pocket and on the MOVIE IDEAS page, scribbled, *Revenge of Frogzilla.*

If Liam was about to protest, he didn't get the time to do so. Amidst a frenzy of putrid froth and bubbles, a hulking and formless mass suddenly hauled itself from the water onto the side of the pool, its mud-lathered and weed-wrapped body slithering and shifting as though attempting to form a shape. Two antennae slid out then retracted again, then two huge lobster claws extended to snap at the air before they too disappeared.

'*What is that?*' asked Liam, ducking lower in the bush.

'Looks like a Blobster,' replied Evan.

'What's one of those?'

'I dunno. Let's find out!'

The creature from the pool continued to reshape itself like a wad of putty, stretching in one direction and then another, a thick steam coming from its foaming skin. Finally it seemed to collapse in on itself, melting to a thin river of green slime that began to wind its way from the pool.

'Come on,' said Evan. 'Let's see what it's up to.'

Liam was much more inclined to run in the opposite direction. But Evan seemed in his element, already in a crouching run with the camcorder held to his eye, like an intrepid cameraman for SCARY TV.

The trickle of gunge snaked onto one of the hotel's outside stairwells, making its way silently up the steps while Evan and Liam followed as close as they dared. When the slime reached the top, it flowed along the terrace past a series of rooms until it came to the last one, where it gathered itself up and forced itself under the door.

'This looks bad,' said Liam.

Evan nodded in agreement, both of them beginning to tiptoe towards the room.

Before they'd got halfway there, the door burst open and a middle-aged man in his pyjamas came fleeing onto the terrace. He looked as though he wanted to scream, but only croaking sounds came from his gaping mouth.

Behind him appeared the Blobster, seething like an angry jelly, various claws and appendages growing and receding from its body as it quickly bore down on its prey. In seconds, it had overtaken the man and wrapped itself around him, making loud squelching noises as it greedily swallowed him. After a large puff of steam and what sounded like a satisfied belch, the creature spat out a pair of slippers and gave a wobble of pleasure.

'Run?' suggested Liam.

But Evan had already gone, his red hair bobbing in the distance. As Liam raced after him, heart in his mouth, he couldn't help but think that Evan could probably be quite good at sports if he wanted to.

When they had reached the safety of their room once more, it took both of them several minutes to catch their breath.

When Evan had finished stuffing a blanket under the door to stop the Blobster sliming beneath it, he watched the camcorder footage he had taken, his face paler than ever as he looked up from the screen.

'I hate to say it,' he announced grimly. 'But I think we could be in trouble.

3. Battle of the Blob

'You don't understand!' protested Liam, as his dad pulled the bath towel away from the bottom of his door. 'We put that there to protect you.'

'Come on, Liam,' scolded his dad, stepping outside the room and locking the door. 'You're going to have to do better than that. We're not leaving, so you'll just have to make the best of things.'

Sophie flipped the pages of a magazine as she leaned against the wall. '*So* lame, Liam,' she tutted, without looking up.

'Excuse me, Mr Brodie,' said Evan, puffing his chest out, 'but as an experienced observer of the paranormal, I feel I must warn you that there is a large, gooey entity on the rampage, and my guess is that it intends to blobbify us all.'

'Blobbify?'

'Well, the process isn't scientifically clear,' said the flustered Evan. 'But it looks *disgusting*.'

'Just try to keep out of trouble you two,' said Liam's dad. 'Sophie and I are going down for breakfast.'

Evan shrugged. 'And that's why monsters get away with it,' he sighed. 'Nobody ever listens.'

'We're not *stupid*, Evan,' said Sophie, stepping past him. 'It's pretty obvious this is just another one of your dumb movies.'

'Better not let it absorb your sister,' muttered Evan to Liam. 'That'd make it slimy *and* bad-tempered.'

Liam and Evan decided to skip breakfast and revisit the grounds. Evan insisted on first applying a tube's worth of sun cream and wearing a large hat.

But once outside, they found the entire hotel in the shadow of an ominous black cloud.

Evan pointed out the vacant-looking guests reclining on loungers around the pool. 'Look at their faces,' he said. 'It's like they're in a trance. I bet they're being fed zombie pills to make them easy victims. Your dad and sister could be next.'

Liam wondered for a moment whether a few zombie pills might not be a bad thing for Sophie.

'We need an advantage,' pondered Evan. 'Something we can use.'

The boys scouted around for a while before Liam spotted a rusty pump in the bushes, its long hose coiled in a heap.

'Perfect!' said Evan, pulling back thorny branches from the pump. 'If we drain the pool the Blobster will have nowhere to go. Without water it'll shrivel up like a raisin. This is our weapon!'

'Could be tricky though,' said Liam, already feeling his bottom cheeks clench in apprehension.

'Fighting supernatural forces is never easy,' said Evan sternly. 'But we're the only ones who can do it.'

Liam was sure there was probably somebody else who could do it if they just asked around a bit, but not wanting to appear a coward, he reluctantly agreed.

The rest of the day passed uneventfully, with both of them doing their best to avoid the hotel manager, who regularly patrolled the grounds, casting a watchful eye over his guests.

When evening arrived, Liam could see that his dad's eyes were already beginning to glaze over, his expression becoming as blank as the guests' by the pool as he pulled on his spiky blonde DJ wig. Time was running out.

Liam turned to his sister, who was engrossed in a thick paperback. 'I'm going on a dangerous mission tonight, sis. If I don't come back, don't try and look for me.'

'Yeah, okay,' she yawned. ''Night.'

When Liam met up with Evan in the deserted grounds, they both looked as nervous as each other.

'What if the pump doesn't work?' asked Liam.

'Then it's Blobbification for both of us,' said

Evan, quietly feeding the hose into the pool.

There was no need to say more; the idea was just unthinkable.

They settled into a hiding place by the pump, both of them relaxing a little as they heard pop songs drifting from the entertainments hall. At least Liam's dad seemed to be doing his best to rouse the guests from their zombified stupor.

Just as Evan had begun to snore, the pool waters finally began to bubble, the familiar eruption beginning.

Liam nudged Evan awake and they tried in vain to start the pump, both of them stabbing desperately at the useless power switch. Aghast, they watched helplessly as the Blobster reduced itself to a thin, slimy trickle and slurped its way up a drainpipe into the hotel.

Liam's eyes widened in alarm as they traced the path of the pipe. 'That's heading to our block!' he yelled.

Within seconds, they had pelted from their hiding position and raced back into the hotel, Evan watching anxiously as Liam banged loudly on his sister's door.

'Sophie, where's Dad? Quick, the Blobster's coming!'

'He's still out,' came the muffled reply. 'I'm in the bath, go away.'

'She's in mortal danger, we can't wait,' panted Evan. He barged against the door and instantly rebounded, clutching his shoulder.

Liam put his full weight behind a charge and burst into the room, only to see Sophie emerging from the bathroom, dressed in a towel and brandishing a solid-looking loofah.

If she was annoyed to see her brother break in, watching Evan follow him was the very last straw.

'I'll give you a horror movie,' she growled, proceeding to batter Evan with her loofah.

Liam ran from room to room, hurriedly stuffing towels into all the taps as Evan huddled into a ball on the floor, Sophie's loofah relentlessly bouncing from his head.

Liam gasped as he saw the green ooze

beginning to emerge from one of the bath taps. He hurriedly thrust a hand towel into the spout, halting its progress.

'We did it!' he said breathlessly, rushing back to Evan. 'We saved her!'

'Yay,' grumbled Evan, rubbing his head.

'We need to get down to the pool!' urged Liam, hurrying from the room.

Evan picked himself up off the floor and groggily followed.

'And don't try and scare me again!' Sophie called after him, standing in the corridor with her loofah.

'We should have just let it in,' huffed Evan, as he caught up to Liam in the grounds. 'Your sister would have beaten it to death.'

Seeing the thin trail of slime emerging from the drainpipe, they scrambled back to the pump and tried once more to start it.

The Blobster arrived at the poolside and reformed for a moment, its antennae twitching, before it sank slowly into the water.

'Wait!' said Liam. 'The power cord is unplugged!' With a rolling lunge, he snatched up the cord and plugged it in. The pump began to hum and vibrate, the hose jerking as pool water surged through it.

Caught immediately by the suction, the Blobster gave a hideous squeal as the hose pulled in its body and forced it through the pump.

Liam and Evan watched in hushed anticipation as the rest of the pool drained, leaving a black and oily pit. The boys held their breath, afraid that the creature might still escape. But the soaking ground behind the pump remained undisturbed.

'Mega!' shouted Evan. 'We kicked its blobby butt!' he whooped, dancing a small victory jig. 'What's wrong with you?' he asked Liam, who wasn't joining in.

The reason soon became apparent, as Evan turned to see the glowering figure of the hotel manager standing over them, the blue pool lights shimmering in his eyes.

'Young fools!' he hissed. 'You have interfered

in something you should not have! Now there will be a terrible price to pay!'

'We thought your pool needed cleaning,' stammered Liam.

'I think we should go,' said Evan.

The two boys hurried from the poolside with the manager's high-pitched shriek echoing around the hotel walls.

'Tomorrow, you will learn your terrible fate,' he screeched. 'Tomorrow you are *doomed*.'

4. Riddle Me This

By the next morning, the boys had decided that leaving the hotel as quickly as possible was the best thing, even if they needed a sneaky plan to achieve it.

'We have a situation,' Liam announced dramatically, opening his bedroom door to his dad and sister as they walked past on their way to breakfast. 'There's something wrong with Evan. I think you'd better take a look.'

Liam's dad stared into the room, where Evan was doing his best to look severely afflicted, tongue lolling out and eyes rolling madly as he thrashed around on the floor.

'I'll say there's something wrong with him,' said Sophie. 'That's the worst acting I've ever seen.'

'I think he's developed an allergy or something,' insisted Liam. 'We need to get him out of here right now.'

'Maybe it's the food,' said Liam's dad. 'I'm not feeling too well myself. I'd better speak to the manager. You kids might as well start packing.'

Sophie waited until her dad had walked off before confronting Liam.

'Okay, so what are you up to?' she demanded.

'Look, we're in big trouble, sis,' explained Liam. 'We sucked up the manager's pet blob and watered the garden with his swimming pool. And now he's going to put a curse on us.'

'Oh no, you don't,' she said, wagging a warning finger. 'I've been tricked into his stupid horror movies before. I'm not falling for it *this* time.'

'But it's not a trick, honest!'

'Sure...'

She slammed the room's door as she left, causing Evan to sit bolt upright.

'*Worst acting ever* indeed!' he said indignantly, wiping the drool from his chin. 'She doesn't know talent when she sees it.'

'Well, I think my dad believed it, and that's what counts. We just need to get out of this place as fast as we can.'

The two boys spent the next hour packing their bags and taking it in turns to stand guard at the door. By the time Liam's dad returned, both of them were flinching at the slightest noise.

'We're leaving,' he told them. 'The manager wasn't pleased, but I told him Evan's ill so there's nothing he could say. You'd better make sure you have all your stuff together, there'll be a taxi here for us in thirty minutes.'

'Fantastic!' said Evan, triumphantly punching his fist in the air before remembering he was supposed to be ill.

By the time they were all ready to leave, a thunderstorm had begun to rage outside, towering forks of lightning splitting the sky while heavy rain lashed the grounds.

For Evan and Liam, standing in the shelter of a covered pathway, the distance to the gates looked a very long one. With the water running in small rivers across the paving, all they could look at was the Blobster-sprayed soil near the bushes, where small bubbles were now beginning to appear.

'I guess we'll have to walk down the hill again,' said Liam.

'We'll get soaking wet!' protested Sophie.

'The taxi driver won't come to the gates!' argued Liam, becoming ever more frantic as he saw small trickles of slime beginning to wind their way over the soil and onto the paving.

'Liam's right,' agreed his dad. 'We'll have to wait at the bottom of the hill. Come on, let's go.'

'Sorry you're leaving so soon,' rasped a shrill voice as they began carrying their luggage across to the gates.

They turned to see the manager hovering behind them, his hands clasped, a look of menace in his frog-like eyes.

'Just one of those things really,' replied Liam's dad, pulling open the heavy iron gates. 'Can't be helped.'

As Evan and Liam made to follow Liam's dad and Sophie through the gates, the manager suddenly grabbed them by their collars, holding both in a vice-like grip as he leaned close to them.

'Soon,' he breathed, 'Barzabalus will have his revenge!'

'B... B... Barzabababalus?' croaked Liam.

'Know that Barzabalus is Gatekeeper of the Netherworld, whose entrance lies beneath the pool you drained. He feeds by sucking souls from the world of humans. And you have offended him!'

'We're very sorry for any inconvenience,' stammered Liam.

'Foolish children! Barzabalus will enter the body of one of you and use it for four days. And then ...' The manager paused for a cruel chortle, '... he will *devour* you both.'

'Seems a bit harsh doesn't it?' protested Evan.

'Can't you at least give us a chance?' pleaded Liam.

The manager paused a moment then lowered his voice to a quiet hiss.

'I'm harder than the thing I'm made of,
more is hidden than you see.
Summer and salt make me to vanish,
whatever could I be?'

And with that, he uttered a malevolent cackle and released them both.

Liam and Evan raced down the hill to join the others.

'You two okay?' asked Liam's dad. 'What did he want?'

'Nothing,' panted Liam. 'He was just being weird again.' He edged closer to Evan and lowered his voice. 'What did he mean by all that "summer and salt" stuff?'

Evan's expression clouded with doom, curtains of rain dripping from his eyebrows and nose.

'I don't know,' he gulped, 'but I think we're already running out of time.'

Both of them peered back up the hill, where the entire ground had begun to swim and ripple as though something were snaking its way towards them in the deluge.

'This looks bad,' said Evan.

When the taxicab appeared through the storm, its headlights blazing funnels through the murk, the two boys could have cheered. With a haste bordering on frenzy, they urged the driver to open the boot and hurriedly stuffed their bags in.

With the sheet of green slime now drawing close, Liam managed to slam his cab door while Sophie climbed in the opposite side.

Evan frantically tried to bundle himself in after her, but his shoe became caught on the door and fell into a puddle. He hesitated for a second, then decided to make a grab for it.

The moment he leaned down, a squishy green slime reared up from the puddle. He squealed in shock as the cold jelly jumped onto his hand, his

sleeve swelling as the ooze slithered all the way up his arm. Sticky tendrils sprouted from it to force their way into his nose and mouth, almost choking him, before disappearing again. Evan fell back in his seat, his eyes wide with shock.

As the cab began to drive away, Liam looked back through the rain to see the faint figure of the manager standing at the top of the hill.

'Everybody all right back there?' asked Liam's dad from the front passenger seat.

Sophie took one look at Evan and made her vomit face. 'I think Evan is turning into a frog,' she said, her nose curling.

Liam scrutinised Evan with growing horror; the boy's already pasty complexion was now almost translucent and riddled with green veins.

'Evan, can you hear me?' he asked.

Evan gazed at him with glazed eyes, his nose and mouth dripping with green goo.

'Anybody got a tissue?' he gurgled.

5. Airport Sludgery

At the airport, Liam bought several large bottles of water which Evan guzzled in quick succession as they sat in the departure lounge.

'Maybe that will flush it out,' he suggested.

Feeling a huge sneeze coming on, Evan tried to hold it in but failed. The resulting storm of sticky, green gunge whirled in the air for an instant before slopping onto the face of a small boy. The child ran wailing to his mother as Evan wiped his mouth in embarrassment.

'Look, we all know what happens when the

hero turns into the monster,' he said miserably. 'You'll just have to finish me off before it's too late.'

'No, there has to be a way out of this! The hotel manager gave us a clue. We just have to solve the riddle.'

'I need to pee,' groaned Evan. 'Prepare for disaster.'

Liam helped him stagger to the toilets, where Evan stumbled into a cubicle.

Hearing the hiss of steam and a dull groan, Liam stepped back in alarm to see a pool of bubbling slime seeping under the cubicle door. Within seconds the small lake had gathered itself up and risen from the tiles, the familiar form of Barzabalus already beginning to materialise.

'*Everyone run for your lives!*' yelled Liam.

As others in the bathroom scattered in panic, the demon snatched a man trying to run with his trousers around his ankles, slurping greedily as it swallowed him up, its claws waving in glee as it spat out his trainers.

When the toilets had emptied, the creature

melted back into a pool and disappeared under the door of Evan's cubicle. After a small shriek and a vile sucking noise, Evan emerged holding the front of his trousers, a pained expression on his face.

'You just *ate* someone!' cried Liam.

Evan burped loudly. 'Oops.'

Liam sighed and shook his head. Doing his best not to look suspicious, he escorted Evan from the toilets and back to the departure lounge, where his dad and Sophie were waiting.

'Is Evan going to be all right?' enquired Liam's dad. 'He looks worse to me.'

'I think he should be quarantined,' said Sophie.

'I'm not a rabid dog!' retorted Evan, frothing at the mouth.

'We just need to get him home,' said Liam. 'Then we can figure out what to do.'

The call to board came just as airport security came rushing into the terminal. Liam quickly helped the stricken Evan to get to his plane seat and then laid a towel over his face, explaining to flight attendants that he needed to sleep off some food poisoning.

But once in the air, Evan quickly dashed any hopes for an uneventful flight when he announced he was feeling airsick.

'Get ready for the mother of all upchucks,' he said wearily.

'Try and get it all in here,' instructed Liam, holding up a tiny paper bag.

Evan looked at him in disbelief then heaved with explosive force, the soaking bag blasting onto the cabin roof, from where it dropped onto a flight attendant's head.

The attendant stood still for a moment, her lips quivering as green sludge began oozing through her hair. A chorus of disgusted groans from passengers prompted her to retreat behind the curtain at the rear of the cabin.

Liam and Evan huddled in their seats and quivered as a furious commotion ensued behind the curtain, a cloud of steam billowing as the attendant's shoes flew into the cabin. They watched in horror as thin trails of slime began to run the length of the cabin, heading towards the plane's cockpit.

'We have to do something!' panicked Liam. 'What if it eats the pilots?'

Rising unsteadily to his feet, Evan put one finger over a nostril and with the other inhaled as hard as he could. In an instant, the rivers of gunge had turned back, gathering under his seat again before flowing as a torrent up his swollen nose.

With a small hiccup, he collapsed back in his seat.

'I'm at maximum snot capacity,' he wheezed, blowing a small green bubble. 'We *have* to solve that riddle.'

'I know,' replied Liam sombrely. 'And we have just four days to do it.'

6. Slime's Up

Mrs Crogan answered the door in her slippers, as usual, and carrying a dirty sponge in her hand.

'He's in his room, Liam, you can go on up,' she said wearily, wiping a spot of slime from her cheek. 'Mind the sludge on the stairs.'

Liam made his way to the stairwell, avoiding the green goo that was staining the carpets and dripping from the ceiling. Little wonder Evan's mum appeared so tired. The official story was that Evan had picked up a cold in Spain, though with school about to start the following day, it seemed that no amount of hot lemon and vitamin C could help.

Liam went into Evan's room and found him slumped in a pool of bubbling sludge, his camcorder pointed at himself.

'Got some good footage, at least,' he said dejectedly. 'Perfect for *Gutgobblers from Mars* – if I ever get to make it.'

'Has it eaten anybody else?' asked Liam.

Evan pointed to a pair of shoes at the bottom of his wardrobe. 'Nobody important. Just a double glazing salesman.'

'Oh, right. Well somebody's going to suspect you soon. They're still looking for that flight attendant from the plane.'

'You haven't worked out the riddle yet?'

Liam shook his head. 'I asked Sophie to help, but she still thinks it's some kind of gag.'

'My mum says I have to go to school tomorrow. She thinks it'll help me feel better.'

'That sounds like a *really* bad idea.'

Evan shrugged. 'Well, I might as well let it eat

the right people. The sports teacher, the football team …'

'Evan, pretty soon it's going to eat *us*! We have to figure this out. Maybe there's something in the chemistry lab we can use to melt it down?'

'Not without melting *me* down,' sighed Evan.

'Hey, don't worry,' said Liam bravely. 'We'll beat it, I know we will. There has to be a way …'

Despite Liam's encouragement, the next morning could hardly have started out worse. With Evan leaving a slimy trail as he entered the school building, Liam could only watch in dismay as Mr Donahue became the first to skid on a slick of demonic gunge.

'Crogan! What on earth do you look like, boy?' demanded the elderly maths teacher, pulling

Evan aside. 'Are you a man or a snail?'

'I've been possessed by a demon, sir.'

'Well that's no excuse for untidiness.' The teacher handed him a clean white handkerchief. 'I suggest you start by blowing your nose.'

'You could be sucked into the Netherworld,' warned Evan.

'You could be sucked into the headmaster's office,' retorted Mr Donahue.

The blast from Evan's nose propelled the maths teacher down the corridor, Liam cowering as the torrent of gunge quickly reformed into the hungry Barzabalus. The lenses of Mr Donahue's glasses steamed over as he was pulled into the creature's swirling innards, the teacher managing one last cry before he was completely enveloped.

'Crogan!! Detennnnttiioonnn!'

Other schoolchildren in the corridor scattered, screaming, before Barzabalus could devour them, leaving the demon to spit out a pair of immaculately polished shoes and a calculator before dissolving again.

'He always gave me rotten grades anyway,' said Evan, with a throaty cackle.

Liam gazed at his friend with alarm.

'This is what I was worried about, Evan. The demon is starting to take over your personality. You're beginning to enjoy it!'

Before Evan had time to protest, Liam had dragged him out of the corridor and into the schoolyard.

'Listen, don't let it gain control,' he urged. 'You have to try to contain it.'

Evan was about to mumble a protest when the tall figure of the headmaster strode into the yard, accompanied by a frightened young girl who pointed both of them out.

'Crogan! Brodie! In my office at once!' shouted the headmaster.

Evan scowled and opened his mouth wide to release a thick jet of slime. The vile-smelling liquid splashed onto the ground, where it immediately began to form the fearsome shape of Barzabalus.

'Evan, no!' cried Liam. 'Don't do it!'

'Too late,' grinned Evan, his eyes narrowing to a menacing squint.

The headmaster took one look at the wobbling bulk that was Barzabalus and began to sprint back across the yard to the school building, the demon following close behind him.

Evan chuckled manically, green saliva dripping from his mouth.

'Evan, I can't believe you did that!' Liam cupped his hands to shout to the fleeing headmaster. 'Sir, run to the chemistry lab!'

'Teacher's pet,' snorted Evan.

Liam ran after Barzabalus, the pursuit taking him back into the school building and up the stairs to the chemistry lab, where he found the door smashed from its hinges. Looking into the classroom, he saw the headmaster trying to squeeze under a desk while the demon seethed and pulsed, its claws waving and snapping at the class of terrified students. And right at the very front, her face tight with fear, cowered Sophie.

'Sis!' cried Liam, running into the room. 'Keep

away from it! Find something to throw!'

Liam dodged around the monster, just out of reach of its claws, as Sophie frantically searched through a cupboard of apparatus and supplies. She picked up a test tube rack and Bunsen burner and hurled them as hard as she could, the demon's body absorbing them as they hit.

'Chemicals!' yelled Liam. 'Throw some chemicals!'

Sophie scanned several labels and grabbed two large, stoppered flasks.

'Don't you dare, young lady!' instructed the chemistry teacher, his bearded face suddenly appearing from behind a desk. 'We don't throw dangerous substances around in *my* class!'

Sophie paused a moment, only for the headmaster to dash forward and snatch the flasks, flinging them at the demon for all he was worth. The chemistry teacher tutted and disappeared again.

The creature's skin began to hiss and foam, its antennae and claws threshing furiously as it began to shrink.

'*Yes!!*' shouted Liam triumphantly. 'We did it!'

Sophie's smile faltered as Barzabalus shook like an electrified blancmange then began to expand again, its body rapidly doubling then tripling in size.

'Oh no, what have we done!?' exclaimed Liam in horror. He grabbed Sophie's hand and bolted from the room, the rest of the class following them.

As they ran back into the yard, the school building was already beginning to shake, a cascade of roof tiles smashing to the ground. To a chorus of gasps, the top of the roof exploded, Barzabalus's wobbling green mass thrusting through it.

'Cool,' sniggered Evan, as everybody else ran for their lives, the side of the school crumbling away.

As Barzabalus's huge mass slithered into the yard, Liam could see the headmaster floating around in its body, his mouth opening and closing fish-like as he pointed an accusing finger.

'See! Now we're both expelled!' Liam shouted to Evan, who didn't look as though he cared very much.

Barzabalus surged across the yard to the sports hall, large panes from its glass roof shattering and falling away as the demon began to crush the building.

'Evan, call it back!' bellowed Liam. 'Hurry!'

Evan simply shrugged as the sports hall collapsed. It wasn't until Sophie had manhandled him to the ground that his arrogance disappeared, a look of fear crossing his face as she drew back her fist.

'Whatever my brother asked you to do,' she shouted, 'you'd better do it *right now!*'

Evan issued a gurgling roar, then drew a huge breath causing the demon to begin shrinking again. Sophie smartly hopped off his chest as a green tide surged across the yard and rushed back into Evan's mouth and nose, leaving him dazed and spluttering.

'*Now* you have to believe me!' Liam pleaded.

Sophie frowned as she picked small lumps of gunge from her hair and flicked them at Evan.

'How did that riddle go again?' she asked, tersely.

7. Supermarket Showdown

'*Harder than the thing I'm made of,*' murmured Sophie to herself, for the umpteenth time. '*More is hidden than you see. Summer and salt make me to vanish, whatever could I be?*'

She stared with bleary eyes at the riddle she had written out then looked across the kitchen table at Liam. 'Are you *absolutely* sure that's what he said?'

'I'm sure,' sighed Liam. 'Come on, sis, it's two in the morning. We're not going to crack it now. I can barely stay awake. Besides, Dad will go nuts if he finds us still up.'

'I thought you said this was the last day?'

Liam nodded dejectedly. 'It is.'

'Then we can't stop trying.' She hopped off her seat and went to the fridge. 'Have a drink, it'll keep you awake.'

'I'll have a Coke,' he mumbled. 'There are some cans in the cupboard. They won't be cold though.'

'That's okay,' replied Sophie, 'I'll put one in the freezer for a couple of m—' She suddenly stopped in her tracks then dashed back to the table to gaze at the words of the riddle again.

'It's ice!' she said triumphantly. 'The answer is ice! Harder than water; more is hidden than you see, like black ice and icebergs. And summer sun and salting roads both dissolve ice!'

Liam sat bolt upright. 'I think you're right,' he exclaimed. 'But how do we beat it with ice?'

Sophie pondered for a moment. 'It's not going to be easy,' she said thoughtfully. 'And we can't let

Evan know what we're going to try. But I have an idea.'

When Liam and Sophie came calling for Evan in the morning his mum was glad to be rid of him for a while. Stained green from head to toe and with her hair fastened up in a net, it looked like she had been scrubbing out a swamp.

'Don't forget your doctor's appointment at twelve,' she reminded him.

'Where are we going?' rasped Evan suspiciously, his voice as hollow as a drainpipe. 'I think you should tell us. We need to know.'

Liam glanced at Sophie, unnerved by Evan's use of 'we' to describe himself. But his sister stayed resolute, her gaze fixed firmly ahead.

'Just thought we'd get some sweets and crisps

from the supermarket,' she said breezily. 'You like those, don't you?'

'No,' snapped Evan. 'We like human souls.'

Liam felt his fists clench as they approached the supermarket. It was important not to think about what they were planning. For all they knew, demons might be able to read minds.

Evan seemed even more wary as they walked down the food aisles, disgusted shoppers pushing their trolleys clear of him as he continued to drool and slobber.

Sophie kept calm as she led them over to the frozen food bays.

'What are you up to?' croaked Evan, 'Are you trying to *trap* us?'

'Now!!' yelled Sophie. 'Quickly!'

Before Evan could react, Liam and Sophie grabbed him and pushed him into one of the deep frozen food bays, his red hair disappearing amongst packets of frozen sausages.

Liam flinched as he heard the familiar roar, a rush of green bile bursting up between the frozen

packets. He was about to let go when the slime slowed to a crawl then stopped altogether, the thick liquid hardening to a brittle, crystalline form.

Sophie pulled a pencil case from her pocket and handed a drawing compass to Liam.

'Quick! Break it up!' she instructed. 'Into little pieces. All of it!'

The gunge continued to freeze and solidify as it left Evan's mouth, Liam and Sophie frantically shattering each new piece as it appeared. Liam hesitated as the supermarket security officer appeared, but before the man had time to say anything, Sophie spun around and swiftly kicked him in a spot that brought tears to his eyes.

As the red-faced officer dropped to the floor, Liam took pity and tossed him a bag of frozen peas.

'Grab a couple of those empty food boxes,' ordered Sophie, still furiously breaking up the pieces of frozen slime with the end of a ballpoint pen.

Liam found himself in awe of his sister – she was acting like a female ninja warrior, just like the ones he'd played in video games. Not that he'd ever tell her that, of course!

He snatched the cardboard boxes up and helped Sophie fill them with the frozen pieces. They pulled Evan from the freezer bay and hurried from the supermarket, leaving the security officer spluttering on the floor.

Liam panted as they ran, the warm sunshine already beginning to melt the lumps in the boxes. Evan staggered behind them, coughing and wheezing, his hands reaching towards the boxes as though seeking to regain a missing twin.

'We're here!' cried Sophie, as they rounded a bend in the road and came across a stretch of roadworks, where fresh tarmac was being laid and steamrollered.

Before the workmen could stop them, Sophie and Liam emptied the boxes onto the steaming tarmac, the pieces of demon sticking to the hot surface. Evan slumped onto his bottom and watched helplessly as the pieces began to swell and froth, each one furiously stretching and pulling to reach another.

'Flatten them!' screamed Sophie to the driver of the steamroller.

The man's eyes were almost popping out of his head.

'Flatten them now, or *I'll* do it!' she threatened.

Stunned into silence, the driver of the steamroller rolled the vehicle forwards to crush the struggling chunks of demon. Liam and Sophie watched nervously as the squashed pieces stopped moving, each of them slowly evaporating into a thick cloud of green steam that billowed outwards, covering the entire road.

When it cleared again, those watching were astonished to see a collection of dazed and bedraggled individuals picking themselves up from the ground. Liam recognised Mr Donahue, the headmaster, the hotel guest, the flight attendant and the man from the airport, as well as other victims he hadn't seen before.

'Wow!' breathed Evan, the green tinge fading from his face. 'It chundered them all back up from the Netherworld. How cool is that?' He began searching his pockets for his MOVIE IDEAS notebook.

The headmaster had recovered enough to point an accusing finger at him.

'Crogan! You are in a *world* of trouble, boy! Be in my office tomorrow at 9 a.m. sharp!'

Liam didn't have the heart to tell the headmaster his office was now a Portakabin. Instead, he patted Evan gently on the shoulder and they walked with Sophie from the scene, leaving the regurgitated victims to search for their missing shoes.

'Well that was intense,' commented Evan, sweeping away the last flecks of slime from his shoulders. 'Though I'd have done it differently if it had been my movie.'

'You're lucky you're still around,' replied Liam, lifting his face up to feel the sun's warmth. 'We both are. And we have one person to thank for that.'

He put his arm around Sophie and squeezed her.

'We'd never have made it without you, sis,' he told her.

'Yeah, nice one, Sophie,' chipped in Evan.

'Maybe a bit over the top on the violence though. We'll have to tone that down a bit in the movie version, make sure the kids can watch it.'

'Here's an idea,' she retorted. 'Don't bother.'

Liam spotted an ice cream van parked by the side of the road. 'How about a celebratory ice cream?' he suggested.

'Seems appropriate,' agreed Sophie.

As the three of them approached the van, a familiar, thin figure leaned from the window, his eyes covered by large sunglasses.

Even with the disguise, all three recognised the hotel manager, and drew to a nervous halt.

The manager broke into a steady clap.

'Well done, well done. You've defeated the Gatekeeper. I'm *impressed*. Would anybody like a treat?'

The manager held out an ice cream cone, but seeing insect legs sticking out of the top, the three of them declined. The manager withdrew the cone and began eating it himself.

'Of course,' he continued, 'there will always be

a Netherworld. And there must always be a Gate-keeper. And so Barzabalus will return. You've challenged this time and won, but next time you may not be so fortunate.' He leaned forward and lowered his sunglasses to reveal his large, fishy eyes. And so my advice to you all,' he concluded, 'is to mind your *own business* next time! Do we understand each other?'

The three of them nodded mutely, leaving the manager to lean back again and lower his shades. Taking a final bite from the ice cream, he flung up both of his spindly hands, and the van collapsed inwards into a tiny series of cubes before vanishing in a plume of black smoke, leaving behind only a vile, farty stink.

'What now?' asked Liam.

'I should apologise to that guy in the supermarket,' said Sophie ruefully. 'And you need to make it up to your poor mother, Evan.'

Evan paused from scribbling in his notebook.

'Hey, I have a great idea for a movie sequel. It starts just where the first story finishes, do you want to hear it?'

REVENGE OF THE BLOBSTER
by Evan Crogan

Several months after being partially demolished by the rampaging demon, Barzabalus, the school building had still not been rebuilt, requiring students to attend the local sports hall and swimming baths for their physical education lessons. During the school cleanup, nobody noticed the small spots of green slime that hung silently in the shadows and in dark corners, and it became common for schoolchildren to unwittingly pick up blobs of slime on their skin and clothes, carrying them beyond the school. By the time the annual swimming competition came around, the local baths had already begun to exhibit the strange phenomenon of bubbling water and a strange green colouration. But only one person knew the signs, knew what to expect and how to face it. And he waited patiently, watched carefully, knowing his time would soon come. His name was Evan Crogan. And he would be known as The Destroyer of Demons ...

Turn the page to read about
more great books from
The O'Brien Press!

THE WITCH APPRENTICE
AND
THE WITCH IN THE WOODS

By Marian Broderick

Anna Kelly is a witch – she can cast spells, brew up magic potions and even transform people into animals. But she's much more interested in sleepovers and hanging out with her friends than practising her magic.

However, there are times when every witch needs to use a little magic ...

The Forbidden Files

Wired Teeth

&

The Poison Factory

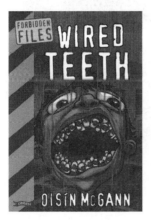 

By Oisín McGann

Crazy dentists, secret agents and remote-controlled braces – welcome to Jason's world in *Wired Teeth*! Find out what the Root Street Gang discover behind the walls of *The Poison Factory* ...

Read all of The Forbidden Files – an exciting series of horrible and bizarre stories.